Includes Compact Disc

SHOO, FLY, DON'T BOTHER ME

Retold by BLAKE HOENA
Illustrated by BRIAN HARTLEY

CANTATA
LEARNING

WWW.CANTATALEARNING.COM

CANTATA LEARNING

Published by Cantata Learning
1710 Roe Crest Drive
North Mankato, MN 56003
www.cantatalearning.com

Library of Congress Control Number: 2015932820
Hoena, Blake
    Shoo, Fly, Don't Bother Me / retold by Blake Hoena; Illustrated by Brian Hartley
    Series: Tangled Tunes
    Audience: Ages: 3–8; Grades: PreK–3
    Summary: How can a tiny, little fly bother a great big cow? Find out in this twist
on the classic song "Shoo, Fly, Don't Bother Me."
    ISBN: 978-1-63290-363-1 (library binding/CD)
    ISBN: 978-1-63290-494-2 (paperback/CD)
    ISBN: 978-1-63290-524-6 (paperback)
    1. Stories in rhymes. 2. Cows—fiction. 3. Farms—fiction.

Book design, Tim Palin Creative
Editorial direction, Flat Sole Studio
Music direction, Elizabeth Draper
Music arranged and produced by Drew Temperante

Printed in the United States of America in North Mankato, Minnesota.
122015   0326CGS16

ACCESS THE MUSIC!

SCAN CODE WITH MOBILE APP

CANTATALEARNING.COM

Cows are usually **calm** animals. Not many things **bother** them. But in this story, a **pesky** fly won't leave one cow alone no matter what she does.

To see what happens, turn the page and sing along!

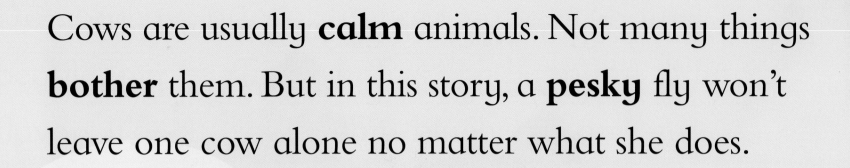

Shoo, fly, don't bother me.
Shoo, fly, don't bother me.

Shoo, fly, don't bother me.
Why'd you have to wake me?

I wish, I wish, I wish you'd go away.

I wish, I wish, I wish you'd go away.

Shoo, fly, stop bugging me.
Shoo, fly, stop bugging me.

Shoo, fly, stop bugging me.
The farmer's here to milk me.

I wish, I wish, I wish you'd go away.

I wish, I wish, I wish you'd go away.

Shoo, fly, don't bother me.

Shoo, fly, don't bother me.

Oh, shoo, fly, don't bother me.

I'm going to the field to feed.

I wish, I wish, I wish you'd go away.

I wish, I wish, I wish you'd go away.

Shoo, fly, don't bother me.
Shoo, fly, don't bother me.

Oh, shoo, fly, don't bother me.
It's time for me to go to sleep!

19

I wish, I wish, I wish you'd go away.

I wish, I wish, I wish you'd go away.

SONG LYRICS
Shoo, Fly, Don't Bother Me

Shoo, fly, don't bother me.
Shoo, fly, don't bother me.

Shoo, fly, don't bother me.
Why'd you have to wake me?

I wish, I wish, I wish you'd go away.
I wish, I wish, I wish you'd go away.

Shoo, fly, stop bugging me.
Shoo, fly, stop bugging me.

Shoo, fly, stop bugging me.
The farmer's here to milk me.

I wish, I wish, I wish you'd go away.
I wish, I wish, I wish you'd go away.

Shoo, fly, don't bother me.
Shoo, fly, don't bother me.

Oh, shoo, fly, don't bother me.
I'm going to the field to feed.

I wish, I wish, I wish you'd go away.
I wish, I wish, I wish you'd go away.

Shoo, fly, don't bother me.
Shoo, fly, don't bother me.

Oh, shoo, fly, don't bother me.
It's time for me to go to sleep!

I wish, I wish, I wish you'd go away.
I wish, I wish, I wish you'd go away.

Shoo, Fly, Don't Bother Me

Hip Hop
Drew Temperante

Verse

1. Shoo, fly, don't both-er me. Shoo, fly, don't both-er me. Shoo, fly, don't both-er me. Why'd you have to wake me?

Refrain

I wish, I wish, I wish you'd go a-way. I wish, I wish, I wish you'd go a-way.

Verse 2
Shoo, fly, stop bugging me.
Shoo, fly, stop bugging me.
Shoo, fly, stop bugging me.
The farmer's here to milk me.

Refrain

Verse 3
Shoo, fly, don't bother me.
Shoo, fly, don't bother me.
Oh, shoo, fly, don't bother me.
I'm going to the field to feed.

Refrain

Verse 4
Shoo, fly, don't bother me.
Shoo, fly, don't bother me.
Oh, shoo, fly, don't bother me.
It's time for me to go to sleep!

Refrain

23

GLOSSARY

bother—to cause trouble

calm—quiet and still

pesky—troublesome

GUIDED READING ACTIVITIES

1. What lands on the cow's nose? Does this bother her? How can you tell? Would it bother you?

2. What does the farmer do in this story? What other things do farmers do?

3. Share something that bothers you. What would you like to "shoo" away?

TO LEARN MORE

Coleman, Miriam. *Flies Eat Poop!* New York: PowerKids Press, 2014.

Esbaum, Jill. *I Am Cow, Hear Me Moo!* New York: Dial Books for Young Readers, 2014.

Meister, Cari. *Farmers*. Minneapolis: Bullfrog Books, 2015.

Smith, Sian. *Flies*. Chicago: Raintree, 2013.